THE CALDECOTT AESOP

Twenty Fables Illustrated by
RANDOLPH CALDECOTT

A Facsimile of the 1883 Edition by
ALFRED CALDECOTT

With an Introduction by
MICHAEL PATRICK HEARN

DOUBLEDAY & COMPANY, INC., GARDEN CITY, NEW YORK

For Justin G. Schiller,
with unlimited respect.
M.P.H.

Library of Congress Catalog Number   77-88424
ISBN 0-385-12653-0 Trade
ISBN 0-385-12654-9 Library

Original edition first published in 1883 by Macmillan and Co., London, England
Introduction Copyright © 1978 by Michael Patrick Hearn

INTRODUCTION

Few works of literature have had so distinguished a history as a source for illustration as have Aesop's fables. These short moralistic tales collectively attributed to a Greek hunchbacked slave have since the Middle Ages been a constant inspiration for artists. Medieval depictions of scenes and characters from the celebrated stories may be found in illuminated manuscript collections or as marginalia in such unexpected places as church psalters and the Bayeux tapestry. With the introduction of printing, the fables were among the first literature to be issued with woodcut decoration. Many masters have displayed their skill in sumptuous volumes, including an Italian translation of 1577 attributed to the Venetian painter Titian. The refinement of copper etching allowed for a freer, more detailed interpretation of the tales with greater emphasis on the naturalistic delineation of the animals and their settings. The sophisticated translations of La Fontaine into French verse inspired a great school of seventeenth- and eighteenth-century fabulists. The most ambitious embellishment of the poems was the rococo edition based upon drawings by Jean-Baptiste Oudry that filled three enormous volumes. Not until the mid-nineteenth century was this impressive interpretation of the fables worthily challenged by the virtuosic wood engravings after designs by Gustave Doré.

One of the first illustrated books to be published in England was the Caxton *Aesop* of 1484. As on the Continent, these animal tales frequently inspired local sporting artists, most notably the émigré Wenceslaus Hollar and his protégé Francis Barlow. Their editions are but two of the extraordinary volumes to display illustrators' affection for the English countryside. The continental influence is evident in the numerous fable books that flourished in London during the Georgian era. John Wootton and William Kent's designs for John Gay's *Fables* (1738) might easily have come from a Parisian studio; but in the Romantic etchings based on this earlier edition, William Blake returned to a more indigenous approach to the subjects. A more localized rural interpretation of the fables was revived in the introduction of white-line engraving by Thomas Bewick who ushered in, not only a new technique, but also a stronger emphasis on the moral content of the texts. In his *Fables of Aesop and Others* (1818), Bewick replaced neoclassical formality with a direct study of nature compatible with the Romantic spirit. By the Victorian age, in those editions of the *Punch* cartoonists John Tenniel and Charles H. Bennett (both followers of the great French caricaturist Grandville), the satiric side of the lessons was more evident than in earlier publications.

THE KID AND THE WOLF—THE FABLE.
Drawn by RANDOLPH CALDECOTT.

A Kid standing on a housetop and seeing a Wolf going by railed and jeered at him. "It is not you, you stupid fellow, who are railing at me," said the Wolf, "but the place you stand on."

From *The English Illustrated Magazine*, vol. 1, 1883.

It was in these grand traditions of British sporting and satiric illustration that Randolph Caldecott produced his unique embellishment of the ancient fables.

Few texts would have been more suited to Caldecott's special talents than Aesop's fables. Born in Chester, Cheshire, in 1846, Caldecott was the son of a shopkeeper but a child of the Midlands. From his early childhood he revealed his deep love for the farmlands, in the sketches he made as he wandered alone through the countryside. He found other means of expression in wood, clay, and paint, but his parents found little future in such interests. At the age of fifteen, the boy was sent to Shropshire to begin a career as a bank clerk. This work did not prove so odious as one might have expected, for it allowed him time to participate in local amusements, in fishing and hunting, and in attending fairs and hound meets. Within a few years, the home office brought him to Manchester, one of the nation's leading commercial centers. Roaming the murky streets, the country lad sketched scenes and characters of local color; and, to amuse himself while in the office, he caricatured customers as they came in and out of the bank. Although he took courses at the Manchester School of Art, Caldecott remained

THE KID AND THE WOLF—APPLICATION.

Drawn by RANDOLPH CALDECOTT.

A country Justice of the Peace bullying an unoffending witness who is personally obnoxious to him.

The "unoffending witness" looks remarkably like Randolph Caldecott, himself.—MPH. From *The English Illustrated Magazine*, vol. 1, 1883.

largely self-taught; and as his comic drawings were slowly being accepted for publication in *The Illustrated London News* and other papers, he abandoned his tenuous life as "a quill-driver" to pursue a spirited career as a free-lance illustrator.

Caldecott's drawings for the popular magazines (such as the *Graphic* and *Punch*) varied from comic studies of contemporary life to rollicking country scenes of fox hunts and other rural sports. In the latter, he particularly excelled with the spontaneity of Thomas Rowlandson and the good humor of John Leech. To one fellow artist, Graham Robertson, Caldecott seemed "a very attractive, charming man and I have pleasant memories of him chiefly in a pink hunting-coat erupting into T.A.'s studio looking very out-of-doors-y and handsome."[1] This impression of robust health was misleading. As Walter Crane recalled in *An Artist's Reminiscences* (1907), Caldecott "never looked strong, and his quiet manner, low voice, and gentle but serious and earnest way of speaking did not suggest the extraordinary vivacity and humour of his drawings." Throughout his life he suffered from a weak heart and tuberculosis; until his death, in Florida, in 1886, nearly forty, his many travels were often as much for his health as for subjects for drawings. Although riding was the only active relaxation permitted him, Caldecott imbued his art as if he were an energetic participant and not merely an astute observer of such sport.

[1] From *The Letters of Graham Robertson*, edited by Kerrison Preston, London, 1953, p. 473.

His first wide recognition as a book illustrator came with the publication of two works taken from Washington Irving: *Old Christmas* (1875) and *Bracebridge Hall* (1877). These popular volumes, illustrated in line and engraved by James David Cooper, reflected the contemporary revival of the Georgian era. Many of the subjects for these essays and those for the *Graphic* anticipated the drawings for his famous picture books, engraved in color by Edmund Evans, from 1878 until his death. It was while working on the Irving books that Caldecott first considered an edition of Aesop. While renting a cottage in Farnham Royal, Buckinghamshire, where the small shed served as a studio, Caldecott made his first sketches of birds and animals that became the basis for the fable illustrations. Cooper suggested as a novelty that a "modern instance," or an example from contemporary life (either political or social), might be attached to each fable as an "application" of the moral. This conception amused the artist, and so his proposed edition embraced both his great affection for the English countryside and his pointed observation of Victorian life.

Apparently Caldecott and Cooper did not immediately engage a publisher for the book, and this work had to be set aside in favor of other assignments. The Society to Promote Christian Knowledge, a prodigious publisher of children's books such as Juliana Horatia Ewing's *Jackanapes* (1883) and other titles illustrated by Caldecott, expressed a desire to see the *Aesop*; but as they had just considered (and returned) Walter Crane's proposal for such a book, Caldecott did not feel comfortable in submitting his version so closely following his friend's rejection.[2] Eventually Macmillan agreed to publish Caldecott's edition.

For its text the artist employed his brother, Alfred Caldecott, a fellow of St. John's College, Cambridge, where he taught English literature, took prizes for political economy, and was noted for his musical compositions. The scholar was obviously not in full sympathy with his brother's handling of the classic material. As indicated by the preparatory note, Alfred hoped to make an authentic translation from the Greek, Roman, and French originals, but Randolph's finished sketches were taken from traditional English retellings which differed in places from the old renderings. As the drawings had been executed some time before the translation, and Randolph was reluctant to submit revisions, the professor succumbed and felt obligated to explain in the preface the discrepancies between the archaic and his new versions.

[2] In a letter to Mrs. Juliana Horatia Ewing, June 6, 1882, *Pictorially Yours, Illustrated letters of Randolph Caldecott,* edited by Michael Hutchins, London and New York, 1976, p. 87. Caldecott was particularly concerned about his friend's feelings as Crane was "sad about a lost baby at present." Crane's edition of the fables, *The Baby's Own Aesop,* appeared in 1887; the S.P.C.K. eventually imported a translation of La Fontaine, illustrated by Maurice Boutet de Monvel.

Due to the artist's poor health, the original scheme for the collection was abandoned in favor of a modified selection of the popular fables. Several drawings dropped from the book were published in *The English Illustrated Magazine*, and eleven unpublished designs were exhibited at the annual show of the students of the Chester School of Art. Caldecott nurtured the possibility of illustrating further volumes, but he objected to subtitling the first collection "1st Selection"; because, as he wrote a friend, "if these don't take, of course I will not trouble the world with others."[3] He admitted he had not taken the subjects too seriously and so the title should be treated accordingly. "I fear," he continued, "that 'select Fables' would suggest a very respectable gathering of highly instructive Fables with morals elegantly and wisely pointed. . . . And I do not want people to be deceived into the notion that they are going to buy all the Fables of Aesop. . . . 'Twenty Fables' would be too auction-like and cause irritable folk to ask 'Why twenty?' 'What twenty?' and to fancy that they are the 20 I like best." The book finally appeared as *Some of Aesop's Fables with Modern Instances*, in the spring of 1883, engraved by J. D. Cooper and bound in a dull pink cloth, stamped in blue. This final title, suggested by the artist, was "more in the spirit of my designs, sketches and scribblings—and yet is not too irreverent—I admit its tendency towards flippancy."

The book did not sell as well as was anticipated. The novelty of the "modern instances" was thought to be in part at fault for the disappointing sales, and perhaps the public, now spoiled by the highly colored picture books, was less willing to purchase a Caldecott collection printed only in line. The publisher re-used the engravings in a cheap school edition of La Fontaine in 1884, but the original volume was popular enough to be reissued in 1887 in a second edition, attractively bound in blue and stamped in gold.

Characteristically Caldecott was disappointed with his efforts. "Do not expect much from this book," he warned a friend. "When I see proofs of it I wonder and regret that I did not approach the subject more seriously."[4] Not everyone agreed with his harsh appraisal of the book. Joseph Pennell, the American etcher and critic, found in the Caldecott *Aesop* the finest examples of the illustrator's "marvellous power in expressing a whole story in a few lines." "It would be impossible," Pennell wrote in *Pen Drawing and Pen Draughtsmen* (1889), "to give a better idea of bounding free motion than in this stag from the *Aesop*, with the whole of Scotland stretching away behind him." The American also admired the laughing fox that fooled the stork, and the lamb before he

---

[3] In a letter to Frederick Locker-Lampson, February 18, 1883, *Pictorially Yours*, p. 239.

[4] Quoted by Henry Blackburn, *Randolph Caldecott: A Personal Memoir of His Early Art Career*, London, 1886, p. 96.

met the wolf: "technically I cannot conceive of anything more innocent and childlike; it would be simply absurd to attempt to copy such a drawing, and yet everything you want is in it." One may easily conclude with Paul Gauguin, when he spoke of Caldecott's animal sketches, "That was the true spirit of drawing."[5]

Surely the *Aesop* is a perfect example of what Caldecott called "the art of leaving out as a science." He argued that "the fewer the lines, the less error committed." This theory should not suggest any carelessness in the planning or execution of the book. Despite his great facility with pen and brush, Caldecott made numerous preliminary sketches for each design in the completed volume. A large collection of these abandoned drawings, mostly for the spot decorations, still survive in the Victoria and Albert Museum. None, however, appears overworked; each is as fresh and spontaneous as a quick thumbnail sketch or a study by a Chinese master. As a comparison between the printed engravings and the original drawings (now in The Houghton Library, Harvard University) proves, J. D. Cooper masterfully preserved in wood the integrity of Caldecott's sketches in brown ink.

The present volume is taken from one of a limited number of hand-colored copies of the first edition. During the nineteenth century, many lavishly illustrated books of Caldecott and others were offered in this special manner, the finest coloring being done in France. John Ruskin was particularly eager to have Kate Greenaway's picture books issued in such editions; he believed that no mechanical process could successfully reproduce such delicate coloring. These special collector's volumes generally carried an extra leaf explaining the nature of the limitation, but none of the hand-colored copies of the Caldecott *Aesop* so far examined contain such a notice. Also as the coloring varies slightly from copy to copy, it has been suggested that these were not issued commercially by the publisher but were probably colored by Caldecott himself for family and friends. The artist often reworked his line drawings (both the originals and proofs) in watercolor. These pages are superior to the commercially facsimiled plates of George Cruikshank and John Leech with their clumsy dabs of red and Prussian blue. Here each design is like a finished watercolor, and one must admit with Ruskin that even the technical expertise of Edmund Evans' engravers could not fully duplicate with their inks the subtleties of the brush. In this new edition of the Caldecott *Aesop,* one may discover nearly a century later this fine example of late Victorian book illustration.

[5] Quoted by A. S. Hartrick, *A Painter's Pilgrimage through Fifty Years,* Cambridge, England, 1938, p. 33.

SOME OF ÆSOP'S FABLES

WITH

MODERN INSTANCES

SOME OF
ÆSOP'S FABLES

WITH

MODERN INSTANCES

SHEWN IN DESIGNS

BY

RANDOLPH CALDECOTT

FROM NEW TRANSLATIONS BY ALFRED CALDECOTT, M.A.

THE ENGRAVINGS BY J. D. COOPER

London
MACMILLAN AND CO.
1883

Printed by R. & R. CLARK, *Edinburgh*.

INDEX

NUMBER		PAGE
I.	THE FOX AND THE CROW	1
II.	THE ASS IN THE LION'S SKIN	5
III.	THE FISHERMAN AND THE LITTLE FISH	9
IV.	THE JACKDAW AND THE DOVES	13
V.	THE COPPERSMITH AND HIS PUPPY	17
VI.	THE FROGS DESIRING A KING	21
VII.	THE DOG AND THE WOLF	25
VIII.	THE STAG LOOKING INTO THE WATER	29
IX.	THE FROGS AND THE FIGHTING BULLS	33
X.	THE LION AND OTHER BEASTS	37
XI.	THE FOX AND THE STORK	41
XII.	THE HORSE AND THE STAG	45
XIII.	THE COCK AND THE JEWEL	49
XIV.	THE ASS, THE LION, AND THE COCK	53
XV.	THE WOLF AND THE LAMB	57
XVI.	THE MAN AND HIS TWO WIVES	61
XVII.	THE FOX WITHOUT A TAIL	65
XVIII.	THE EAGLE AND THE FOX	69
XIX.	THE OX AND THE FROG	73
XX.	THE HAWK CHASING THE DOVE	77

NOTE.

SIXTEEN of these Twenty Fables have been handed down to us in a Greek form: for these Halm's text has been used. As to the other four—Number IX. is from Phaedrus, and retains a flavour of artificiality; Numbers XIII. and XX. are from Latin versions; and Number X. is from a French one.

The Translations aim at replacing the florid style of our older English versions, and the stilted harshness of more modern ones, by a plainness and terseness more nearly like the character of the originals.

In the following cases the Translations have been adapted to the Designs. In Number I. *cheese* has been put for *meat;* in Number VIII. a *pack of Hounds* for a *Lion;* in Number XI. a *Stork* for a *Crane;* in Number XIX. a *Frog* for a *Toad;* and in Number VII. the Dog should be *tied up.* The reason for this is, that in the collaboration the Designer and Translator have not been on terms of equal authority; the former has stood unshakeably by English tradition, and has had his own way.

A. C.

THE FOX AND THE CROW

THE FOX AND THE CROW.

A CROW stole a piece of cheese and alighted with it on a tree. A Fox watched her, and wishing to get hold of the cheese stood underneath and began to make compliments upon her size and beauty; he went so far as to say that she had the best of claims to be made Queen of the Birds, and doubtless it would have been done if she had only had a voice. The Crow, anxious to prove to him that she did possess a voice, began to caw vigorously, of course dropping the cheese. The Fox pounced upon it and carried it off, remarking as he went away, "My good friend Crow, you have every good quality: now try to get some common sense."

THE ASS IN THE LION'S SKIN

THE ASS IN THE LION'S SKIN

AN Ass who had dressed himself up in a Lion's skin was mistaken by everybody for a lion, and there was a stampede of both herds and men. But presently the skin was whisked off by a gust of wind, and the Ass stood exposed; and then the men all charged at him, and with sticks and cudgels gave him a sound drubbing.

THE FISHERMAN AND THE LITTLE FISH

THE FISHERMAN AND THE LITTLE FISH.

A FISHERMAN cast his net and caught a little Fish. The little Fish begged him to let him go for the present, as he was so small, and to catch him again to more purpose later on, when he was bulkier. But the Fisherman said: "Nay, I should be a very simpleton to let go a good thing I have got and run after a doubtful expectation."

THE JACKDAW AND THE DOVES.

THE JACKDAW AND THE DOVES.

A JACKDAW observing how well cared for were the Doves in a certain dovecote, whitewashed himself and went to take a part in the same way of living. The Doves were friendly enough so long as he kept silence, taking him for one of themselves; but when he once forgot himself and gave a croak they immediately perceived his character, and cuffed him out. So the Jackdaw, having failed in getting a share of good things there, returned to his brother Jackdaws. But these latter not recognizing him, because of his colour, kept him out of their mess also; so that in his desire for two things he got neither.

THE COPPERSMITH AND HIS PUPPY

THE COPPERSMITH AND HIS PUPPY

A CERTAIN Coppersmith had a Puppy. While the Coppersmith was at work the Puppy lay asleep; but when mealtime came he woke up. So his master, throwing him a bone, said: "You sleepy little wretch of a Puppy, what shall I do with you, you inveterate sluggard? When I am thumping on my anvil you can go to sleep on the mat; but when I come to work my teeth immediately you are wide awake and wagging your tail at me."

THE FROGS DESIRING A KING

THE FROGS DESIRING A KING

THE Frogs were grieved at their own lawless condition, so they sent a deputation to Zeus begging him to provide them with a King. Zeus, perceiving their simplicity, dropped a Log of wood into the pool. At first the Frogs were terrified by the splash, and dived to the bottom; but after a while, seeing the Log remain motionless, they came up again, and got to despise it so much that they climbed up and sat on it.

Dissatisfied with a King like that, they came again to Zeus and entreated him to change their ruler for them, the first being altogether too torpid. Then Zeus was exasperated with them, and sent them a Stork, by whom they were seized and eaten up.

THE DOG AND THE WOLF

THE DOG AND THE WOLF.

A WOLF, seeing a large Dog with a collar on, asked him: "Who put that collar round your neck, and fed you to be so sleek?" "My master," answered the Dog. "Then," said the Wolf, "may no friend of mine be treated like this; a collar is as grievous as starvation."

THE STAG LOOKING INTO THE WATER

THE STAG LOOKING INTO THE WATER

A STAG parched with thirst came to a spring of water. As he was drinking he saw his own reflection on the water, and was in raptures with his horns when he observed their splendid size and shape, but was troubled about his legs, they seemed so thin and weak. As he was still musing, some huntsmen with a pack of hounds appeared and disturbed him, whereupon the Stag took flight, and keeping a good distance ahead so long as the plain was free from trees, he was being saved; but when he came to a woody place he got his horns entangled in the branches, and being unable to move was seized by the hounds.   When he was at the point of death he said to himself: "What a fool am I, who was on the way to be saved by the very things which I thought would fail me; while by those in which I so much trusted I am brought to ruin."

THE FROGS AND THE FIGHTING BULLS

THE FROGS AND THE FIGHTING BULLS

A FROG in his marsh looking at some Bulls fighting, exclaimed: "O dear! what sad destruction threatens us now!" Another Frog asked him why he said that, seeing that the Bulls were only fighting for the first place in the herd, and that they lived quite remote from the Frogs. "Ah," said the first, "it is true that our positions are wide apart, and we are different kinds of things, but still, the Bull who will be driven from the rule of the pasture will come to lie in hiding in the marsh, and crush us to death under his hard hoofs, so that their raging really does closely concern the lives of you and me."

THE LION AND OTHER BEASTS

THE LION AND OTHER BEASTS.

THE Lion one day went out hunting along with three other Beasts, and they caught a Stag. With the consent of the others the Lion divided it, and he cut it into four equal portions; but when the others were going to take hold of their shares, "Gently, my friends," said the Lion; "the first of these portions is mine, as one of the party; the second also is mine, because of my rank among beasts; the third you will yield me as a tribute to my courage and nobleness of character; while, as to the fourth,—why, if any one wishes to dispute with me for it, let him begin, and we shall soon see whose it will be."

THE FOX AND THE STORK

THE FOX AND THE STORK.

THE Fox poured out some rich soup upon a flat dish, tantalising the Stork, and making him look ridiculous, for the soup, being a liquid, foiled all the efforts of his slender beak. In return for this, when the Stork invited the Fox, he brought the dinner on the table in a jug with a long narrow neck, so that while he himself easily inserted his beak and took his fill, the Fox was unable to do the same, and so was properly paid off.

"With Mr Fox's respects &
many happy returns of the day"

"With Mrs Stork's kind regards
and the compliments of the season"

THE HORSE AND THE STAG

THE HORSE AND THE STAG.

THERE was a Horse who had a meadow all to himself until a Stag came and began to injure the pasture. The Horse, eager to punish the Stag, asked the man whether there was any way of combining to do this. "Certainly," said the Man, "if you don't object to a bridle and to my mounting you with javelins in my hand." The Horse agreed, and was mounted by the Man; but, instead of being revenged on the Stag, he himself became a servant to the Man.

THE COCK AND THE JEWEL

THE COCK AND THE JEWEL.

A BARN-DOOR Cock while scratching up his dunghill came upon a Jewel. "Oh, why," said he, "should I find this glistening thing? If some jeweller had found it he would have been beside himself with joy at the thought of its value: but to me it is of no manner of use, nor do I care one jot about it; why, I would rather have one grain of barley than all the jewels in the world."

THE ASS, THE LION, AND THE COCK

THE ASS, THE LION, AND THE COCK.

AN Ass and a Cock were in a shed. A hungry Lion caught sight of the Ass, and was on the point of entering the shed to devour him. But he took fright at the sound of the Cock crowing (for people say that Lions are afraid at the voice of a Cock), and turned away and ran. The Ass, roused to a lofty contempt of him for being afraid of a Cock, went out to pursue him; but when they were some distance away the Lion ate him up.

THE WOLF AND THE LAMB

THE WOLF AND THE LAMB.

A WOLF seeing a Lamb drinking at a brook, took it into his head that he would find some plausible excuse for eating him. So he drew near, and, standing higher up the stream, began to accuse him of disturbing the water and preventing him from drinking.

The Lamb replied that he was only touching the water with the tips of his lips; and that, besides, seeing that he was standing down stream, he could not possibly be disturbing the water higher up. So the Wolf, having done no good by that accusation, said: "Well, but last year you insulted my Father." The Lamb replying that at that time he was not born, the Wolf wound up by saying: "However ready you may be with your answers, I shall none the less make a meal of you."

THE MAN AND HIS TWO WIVES

THE MAN AND HIS TWO WIVES.

A MAN whose hair was turning gray had two Wives, one young and the other old. The elderly woman felt ashamed at being married to a man younger than herself, and made it a practice whenever he was with her to pick out all his black hairs; while the younger, anxious to conceal the fact that she had an elderly husband, used, similarly, to pull out the gray ones. So, between them, it ended in the Man being completely plucked, and becoming bald.

THE FOX WITHOUT A TAIL

THE FOX WITHOUT A TAIL.

A FOX had had his tail docked off in a trap, and in his disgrace began to think his life not worth living. It therefore occurred to him that the best thing he could do was to bring the other Foxes into the same condition, and so conceal his own deficiency in the general distress. Having assembled them all together he recommended them to cut off their tails, declaring that a tail was an ungraceful thing; and, further, was a heavy appendage, and quite superfluous. To this one of them rejoined: "My good friend, if this had not been to your own advantage you would never have advised us to do it."

"Nonsense, my dears! Husbands are ridiculous things & are quite unnecessary!"

THE EAGLE AND THE FOX

THE EAGLE AND THE FOX.

AN Eagle and a Fox entered into a covenant of mutual affection and resolved to live near one another, looking upon close intercourse as a way of strengthening friendship. Accordingly the former flew to the top of a high tree and built her nest, while the latter went into a bush at the foot and placed her litter there. One day, however, when the Fox was away foraging, the Eagle, being hard pressed for food, swooped down into the bush, snatched up the cubs and helped her own fledglings to devour them. When the Fox came back and saw what had happened she was not so much vexed at the death of her young ones as at the impossibility of requital. For the Eagle having wings and she none, pursuit was impossible. So she stood some distance away and did all that is left for the weak and impotent to do—poured curses on her foe. But the Eagle was not to put off for long the punishment due to her violation of the sacred tie of friendship. It happened that some country-people were sacrificing a goat, and the Eagle flew down and carried away from the altar some of the burning flesh. But when she had got it to her eyrie a strong wind got up and kindled into flame the thin dry twigs of the nest. So that the eaglets, being too young to be able to fly, were roasted, and fell to the ground. Then the Fox ran up and, before the Eagle's eyes, devoured them every one.

THE OX AND THE FROG

THE OX AND THE FROG.

AN Ox, as he was drinking at the water's edge, crushed a young Frog underfoot. When the mother Frog came to the spot (for she happened to be away at the time) she asked his brothers where he was. "He is dead, Mother," they said; "a few minutes ago a great big four-legged thing came up and crushed him dead with his hoof." Thereupon the Frog began to puff herself out and asked whether the animal was as big as that. "Stop, Mother, don't put yourself about," they said; "you will burst into two long before you can make yourself the same size as that beast."

*"There, my child, have I not as many buttons
as Lady Golderoy now?"*

THE HAWK CHASING THE DOVE

THE HAWK CHASING THE DOVE.

A HAWK giving headlong chase to a Dove rushed after it into a farmstead, and was captured by one of the farm men. The Hawk began to coax the man to let him go, saying that he had never done him any harm. "No," rejoined the man; "nor had this Dove harmed you."